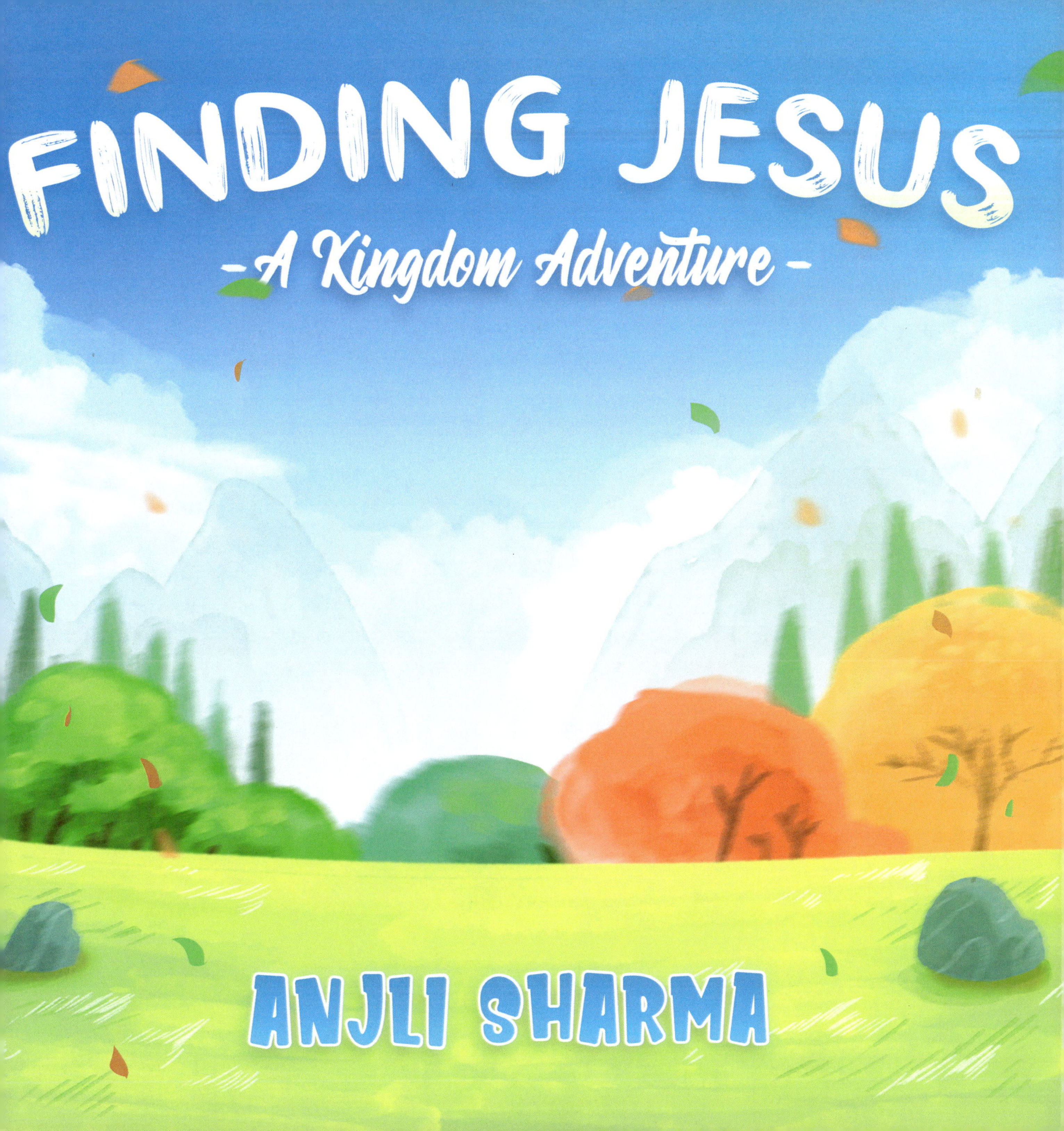

FINDING JESUS
-A Kingdom Adventure-
ANJLI SHARMA

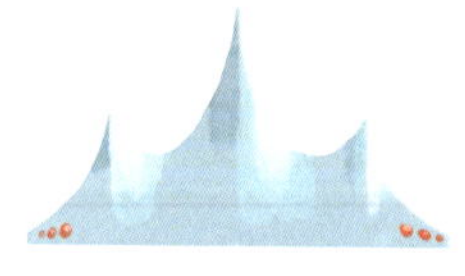

2020 Anjli Sharma

ISBN: 979-8-695-87109-8 (paperback)
ISBN: 978-0-578-78309-3 (hardcover)

First Edition Book, October 2020

Book cover design, illustration, editing, and interior layout by:
1000 Storybooks

www.1000storybooks.com

Dedication

I dedicate *Finding Jesus* to God. He gave me the vision of writing this children's book, and it has been such a blessing. This book is also dedicated to children everywhere who are looking for someone to comfort and encourage them when life gets tough. May they meet the Jesus written about in these pages.

Habakkuk 2:2 (NIV) "Then the Lord replied: 'Write down the revelation and make it plain on tablets so that a herald may run with it.'"

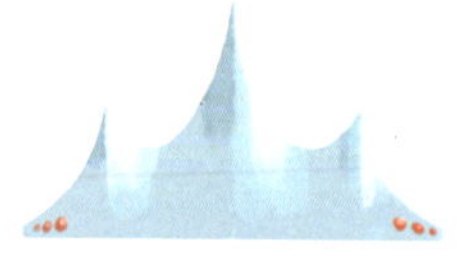

Once upon a time there was a beautiful Indian princess named Riya who lived in a far away palace in Rajasthan, India. She was engaged to marry a handsome Indian prince named Raj TOMORROW!

She had been planning her wedding with Raj for a whole year! There were so many flowers. Every color you can imagine! There was gold and shining emeralds hanging from the ceiling, a long red carpet, and even an elephant with colorful paint on his face!

She was so excited. How would she sleep?!

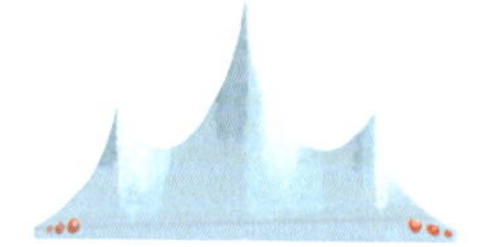

When she awoke the next morning there was a note laying right next to her pillow. Her hands were shaking as she ripped the letter open to discover the day's first big surprise!

It was from Prince Raj, hooray!

She opened it up, and she couldn't believe what it said. Her heart sank down into her toes...

My Dearest Riya,
I am so sorry, but i will not be marrying you today.
It's not you, it's me.
-Raj

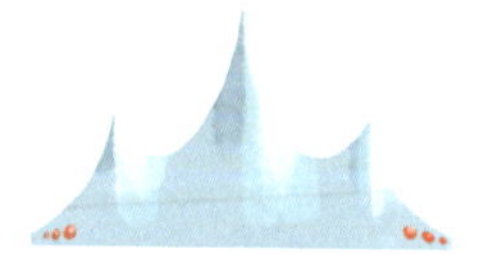

Riya felt her heart break in half. It hurt so bad she thought it would explode!

She rushed all over town to ask different people to help heal her broken heart, but none of the sorcerers, witches, or wizards were able to help her.

She ran into a dark alley, sat down in the dirt, put her face in her hands, and filled them with tears.

Worst day ever!

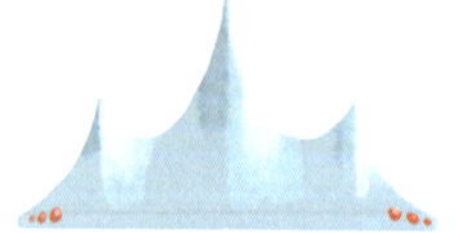

She needed something to heal her hurting heart, so she decided to pack her bags and leave the palace without saying a word to her family.

Outside of the palace walls, Para, her magical white unicorn awaited her. Princess Riya jumped on and together they rode! Her heart was still sad, and she had no peace.

She didn't pay attention to where Para was taking her. She just kept her arms wrapped tightly around Para's neck as she galloped for days and nights through strange lands.

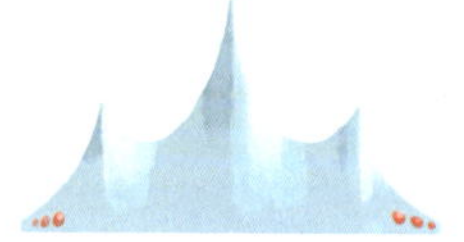

On the morning of the third day, Princess Riya woke up when a big splash of water hit her in the face. Para was swimming out to a beautiful Paradise Island. Unicorns are amazing! It looked like a perfect place to rest.

Para felt very thirsty, so she drank some water from the sea.

Princess Riya jumped off Para's back onto the beach and saw the name JESUS written on the sand, and immediately she wondered what it meant. Was it the name of a local tribe? Was it the name of the beach? A type of food? She had no idea, but she was curious to find out. There seemed to be something quite magical about it.

JESUS

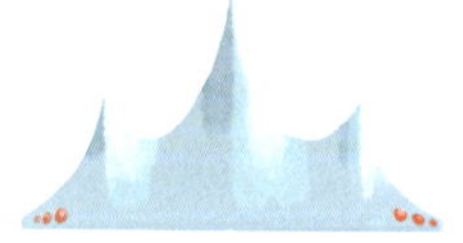

Riya and Para continued on their journey.

Next they arrived in Jumbo Jungle where there were lots of trees and fruits. Princess Riya grabbed the biggest, juiciest apple she had ever seen, but just as she was about to eat it, she saw the name JESUS again! This time it was written on a leaf.

She wondered again, What is JESUS?

Again, she felt a strange, warm feeling in her chest that made the pain better for a few minutes. She had to find more about Jesus to cure her broken heart!

JESUS

Princess Riya and Para continued searching for this Jesus thing and soon they came to the Dangerous Desert.

 There they saw camels walking by. Princess Riya leaned over and whispered to Para.

"Where do you think they are going?"

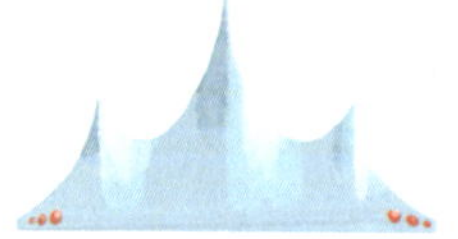

So Princess Riya decided to approach an old man on one of the camels.

"Hi, um, excuse me! Where are you going, Sir, and, um, what's with the camels?"

He answered with a warm smile, "We are going to see the Prince of Peace, Jesus. These camels have boxes of gifts for him."

"Perfect! That's exactly what, I mean who, I was hoping to find. Prince of Peace! Music to my ears! Can I come with you?"
"Of course my dear, follow us."

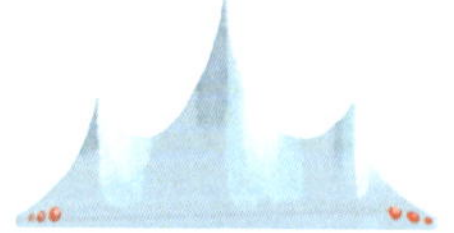

Princess Riya and Para followed the old man and the camels, and they arrived in a town with a lot of lights, houses, and a maze of dusty streets.

She saw people shopping in the streets and wondered how much farther the camels were going.

After days of riding on a unicorn's back her heart wasn't the only thing hurting!

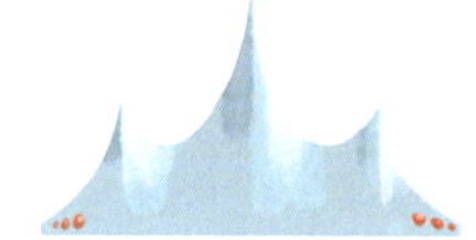

The old man stopped at a house full of lights and said to Princess Riya,

"This is where Jesus lives. He lives here in this house."

Princess Riya was very excited, so she put on her best friendly face to meet him.

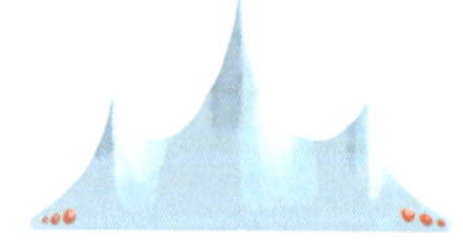

She saw him eating dinner with his family. Jesus noticed her, put his fork down and said, "Hello there girl. Have you come to see me?"

"Yes Jesus. I need serious help."

Jesus asked, "How can I help you?"

"Well there was this guy. A prince and all. And I was supposed to get married. But I woke up and there was a note. And, and... Well I totally have a broken heart., Can you fix it?"

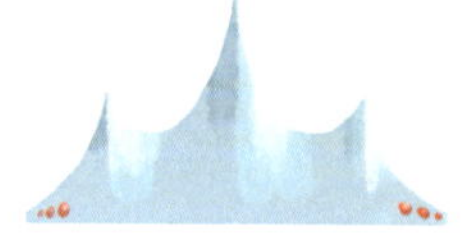

Jesus was calm. He simply stretched out his arm with his fingers slightly apart. Riya got quiet and just looked up into his eyes. It was like looking up at the stars on a dark night. And in a gentle but strong voice he said,

"Be healed, my child. You will now be free to carry on!"

Princess Riya felt warmth in her chest and felt her heart come back together whole and then open up like a butterfly spreading its wings. Then she spread her arms up to the sky and said,

"There is no one like Him! He is the Lord Jesus that has healed my heart and set it free!"

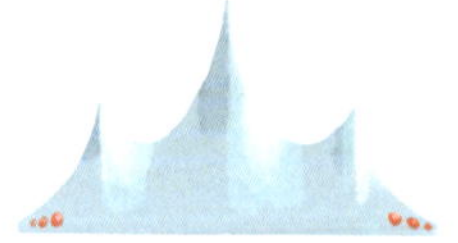

Princess Riya thanked Jesus and rode Para back to the palace immediately to tell her entire royal family about Jesus.

They thought she was crazy.

She and Para left the palace again, because her family didn't want to believe in Jesus. She left to go back to the village to see Jesus a second time, only to hear people in the village talking about how Jesus had died while she was gone!

Princess Riya felt her heart breaking again.

Riya and Para raced to Jesus's home to ask his family what happened. They said He died on a cross, but three days later the tomb was found empty. He rose from the dead on the third day! Jesus was alive again!

She was so excited to hear that Princess Riya prayed for Jesus to heal her once more.

After praying, Princess Riya found Jesus and his peace a second time. From then on, she lived praying to Jesus and telling other people about how Jesus restored, healed, and brought her everlasting love.